A Murderous Mystery

A Murderous Mystery

Queenie D'Souza

ISBN 13: 978-93-90507-43-6
ISBN 10: 93-90507-43-X

Printed in India and published by BUUKS.

Dedication

To my dearest dad, Late Vincent M. D'Souza Prabhu

Part 1

IT WAS ON January 5th, 2020, after attending my nephew's first birthday party, I came home zapped. That evening I met one of my old friend's after a decade for a coffee. We spoke for hour's until I received a call from my mum that my baby would wake up anytime and it would be better if I came home sooner. She is my first priority always. I reach home and get welcomed with laughter and hugs from my little girl. Her energy is contagious enough to come back from a lost world. She stood as my only hope at that given time.

Covid 19 news made the rounds on TV channels and social media around this time. Like most of you, I was quite sure this virus was going to murder many of us. It murdered my thought process, emotions, reasoning capacity and freedom. To me it was the end of my happiness, beginning of anxiety and paranoia. Nothing could possibly deter me from resolving these serious mental blocks.

End of the month I startled when my baby refused to have her food and water. My husband working in the Middle East while I am in India along with my 75 year old mom, I wondered what can I do now? I felt so wretched, with my thoughts gushing over. I booked a cab to my friend's mum's home so to find some calm. To my mum and baby it certainly was a big change as those few minutes spent here gave her some relief – less for her to deal with my banter! My mind and heart were just not in synchronisation and kept losing its plot with whatever I was dealing with, for no definite reasons. The following day I booked an appointment with a pediatrician. After examining my child, he smiles and says – "A very mild throat infection." Ah! My little girl has to inherit my childhood traits when it comes to dietary habits is what I thought to myself.

My little darling,
With a heart so pure,
Come what may,
You are my only cure.

Part 2

FEBRUARY 9TH 2020, my mum turned 76 year's old. I cooked authentic Manglorean dishes, ordered a cake, invited my friend's mum to have this day celebrated. This kept me busy and brought me out from a phase that I was stuck. Woefully it only lasted for a day.

I loved the sunny morning's, noisy afternoon's and dreaded those lonely evening's, quiet night's. It is often said that if a person cannot enjoy being alone, it greatly signifies that we do not appreciate and love ourselves enough. I murdered myself at every chance that I had to live those alone moment's. Evening walks were filled with disastrous feelings and my heart lived in fear as night approached.

One of the early morning's, my friend had a conversation with me on Whatsapp. He randomly told me about his observation on January 5th – If there was something that is bothering me, I could share with him, assuring me that it will be kept as a secret. I wish I could share, I wish I had reasons, I wish there was something clear – but my heart was blank with no issues and my mind had gruesome thoughts which murdered my soul.

My mind lost its charm,
Dreams bewildered,
With all the gifts, God blessed me with,
My thoughts hindered.

I wore a mask of fakeness.

I would fake my smile, my happiness, vulnerability, my whole being, because I believed the world would never accept, if I wore my heart on my sleeve.

The days seemed to be more burdened with anxiety.

But there is something positive in everything that's going wrong. I do get overtly excited with what seems silly to the rest. My happiest moment during this period was to receive my driving license. I daydream a lot! As I took a walk after collecting my license, I kept visualising myself driving around the city. But this time even my day dreaming gave up on me. It was the shortest moment of joy and the feeling of melancholy continued.

I am still a dreamer because it lets me think beyond and it contains an artistic power to get things done quickly.

Part 3

MARCH 24TH 2020 was the first day of a nationwide lockdown in India and the last day of my evening walk. It was a day that was filled with emotions of fear and uncertainty on where will the cycle of murder lead to. I began to picture this deadly virus. Although one can see under an electron microscope, my eyes had a better view of this murderer. My subconscious mind had pictured this as brutal and one which wanted to kill my soul. My heart was infuriated as it was buried with seeds of animosity.

We already had a first Covid case in our city by this time. All I felt was a sense of displeasure. I bitterly cried as I spoke to a friend over the phone. With days passing by everyone were leading their normal lives with enthusiasm except me!

To live within these four walls of my own sweet home, seemed to be a tragedy.

Looking out from my balcony to click some photos as I laid my eyes on the picturesque scenery became my luxury. Morning's were filled with its own kind of amusement, watching people maintaining a certain distance as they waited outside the grocery shops wearing face masks. Some were bluish, pink, multi-colored and of various shapes and styles! I had never experienced this sense of discipline in obeying any other law. Perhaps a fine that would be imposed for not wearing a face mask became a big deal for a lot of them.

The most striking coincidence was that of me wearing a mask from October 2019. This was much before the virus made its announcement. People around kept staring at me like I am an alien, passersby teasing as they found something to joke about. I was called – "That girl who wears a mask." However this was a strong choice to save myself from people who were clueless about their actions of them sneezing and coughing on my face. This also has a story larger than your imagination, a anxious heart which only wanted to protect herself and her little one. My daughter had got infected with sepsis and miraculously healed with no major health issues, under the guidance of her pediatrician. I later felt the necessity of protecting myself and be mindful of certain habits.

This phase taught me to never judge people and accept them as they are.

To be kind, because I do not know what their story is.

I had my own trials and tribulations.

So now I am aware,

And I keep my thoughts still,

Sinking in silence,

My mind whispering it's healing prayer's.

This was a privilege I got to see during my own storm on how karma works.

Hundreds laughing at you,

One day you smile from a distance,

To know they are now following you.

I took this as a life changer. This whole experience taught me to be compassionate and kind. Do my own thing, do it with goodness and let others live. Shine and let others shine.

Part 4

WHILE EVERY NEW day has its challenges, I faced the next day with a need of expressing my true self to few of them. I shared my thoughts, anxiety and worries. Advices that I had never asked for kept pouring in, with no listening ear. Although I was busy running errands and my whole self in a bustling world, with a sweetest toddler I was on my toes. To accept that no one understands was more devastating than what I was actually going through. It became a constant battle.

I wanted to scream out loud and tell the world to imagine with their eyes closed of what it feels like to see someone's waiting for them at the door to knock them down. But I know most of them would feel nothing. People wanted to convince me that I have a mental block, I was a foolish scary bird and a weak hearted person. Finally I gave up accepting the fact that no one cares.

Fortunately, none of you have the liberty to drag me to a loony bin. I bet I'd write better in a surrounding that is filled with madness. Highly censorious and merciless crowd limits my thinking. The world speaks of vulnerability but we are scared of it, because this sounds like truth and feels like courage. So we ignore ourselves and try to put on our happy face without feeling good within.

We have more machines and less humans. We have smartphones with less smart people.

With all of this, I do admire the fearlessness of people who defeated the murderer with their carefree attitude. Some clearly had no choice unlike the rest (like me) who could decide for themselves. Hats off to the one's who managed their daily routine as if nothing was wrong.

Cracked palms,
Anxious mind,
Feeble body,
Confused soul,
Dead heart!

This was simply me with the feeling of emptiness in my whole being. Hoping for a miracle, remained in vain.

Part 5

AS WE WERE approaching towards the month of June, I blinked my eyes and smiled at the rising sun. I had a reason to be thankful for as it was my birthday month. Whatsoever happens, this month stands unique. It reminds me of the most beautiful blessing called 'life' for which I am ever grateful for. It takes me back to my childhood and teenage year's! My mum and dad would celebrate my life with enthusiasm. To them I was the most precious one. It is because of their vigorous joy, I have learnt to appreciate my own presence in this world. More than a million people living on this planet will not wake up every single day. So being alive to this day is a greater blessing.

Age is just a number. It is just a figure that ascends every year so to be grateful to our Creator for giving us an opportunity to execute our dreams. I feel younger every passing year and this feeling in me supercedes all the chaos that is going on. This attitude remains unequivocal.

Many a times people ask me, if I will ever grow or remain a kid for a lifetime? Few others feel I have been over pampered by my parent's! My excitement towards anything small, makes most of the people think it is silly. Probably they take life too seriously and this time I took the pandemic more seriously than the rest. They misunderstand sweetness and kindness to childishness. We just don't click.

I give a sarcastic smile in confusion, questioning them in my mind what does it mean to grow?

To them it is to gossip about somebody else's daughter or son, someone's house been painted because of a wedding, if the neighbor's wife had a C-section or a normal delivery, if that mother is breastfeeding or bottle feeding her newborn, if that young boy earns a 4 or a 5 figure salary, a girl's character, keen on why those youngsters chose to elope, material status of somebody else, why the wife and husband live in 2 different countries, etc!!!

Wow! What a matured mind unlike mine which I will forever fail to understand and get along.

I find myself nowhere wrong in not being a part of kitty parties, in not following a typical mentality where a daughter-in-law has to live with her in-law's and nothing wrong in hanging out with friend's for a coffee or go trekking. Rules are man made and I am born to either delete or mend those.

So I remain a kid with more liveliness and loneliness, because most of them never ever want to be a part of creative and fun conversations anymore. I choose not to change the definition of my personality, just to fit in this society.

It is good to be standing alone until I find my tribe and be as happy as a kid waiting to forward the pictures of a lovely blue sky and chocolates I love, music that I listen to, novels I read, silliest doodles drawn, messy hall with toys on the floor, funny faces clicked of my baby and me, dancing my heart out when I know I will be heading to a beach.

Talk to me about your hobbies, love, friendship, heartbreaks, worries, crushes, your dream job, accomplishments, talents, art, fears, fun... I keep it real as I am a child at heart and an adult with responsibilities. To still be high- spirited and live in liberty has been my uniqueness. It defines my personality, gives me the privilege to have fewer friend's with a deeper connection. I know it is a brief life and I am mortal. I find no time to do anything gibberish, which would mean nothing to me. I am aware that I have a very limited amount of time to make the best things that I truly care to do.

Part 6

ON JULY 7TH 2020, my precious girl turned 3! It is my miraculous day for inexplicable reasons. I had our home decorated with balloons and unicorns, delicious food on the table, gifts well packed and a gorgeous self baked cake done while she was fast asleep. My birthday girl woke up flabbergasted and stunned. It is quite a task to impress this tiny human. This tiny body has a whole lot of imagination and intelligence carried within. I see beauty and brilliance all wrapped together which makes her a strong willed child. She is the one I prayed for and to watch her grow in confidence and having a strong personality makes me feel proud. This day had it's own charm and dazzling moment's to cherish.

I feel it is necessary that we protect our child's imagination and innocence. Let a child be a child. Let that child grow in freedom and create a beautiful world of their own. We are too burdened that we think this life is a rat race. By pulling out our own insecurities we push these kids to do something which the society wants them to do. By not giving them a chance to express and feel, we create another machine out of a tiny lively human!

I let my girl,
Break the norms,
Learn from her mistakes,
Scribble those walls,
Feel the sound,
Express her anger,
Show love,
Cry out loud,
Do what she feels like doing.

She brings hope and she is my best teacher for life. Her existence has made me feel better about myself.

Part 7

DOES THE SUN shine bright forever?

I knew this phase had something unusual in store for me. I had to let go of toxic people from my life which required me to be firm and gentle with myself. I was emotionally drained. When few people in our lives show the phenomenon of their mistakes from the past and live in guilt, anger and revenge, their existence is only filled with bitterness. You realise at some point that their traits have showed up on you and darkness engulfed from within.

I had a ball of emotions which made me go against my own family. It was time to have these feelings released. Harder to let go of these toxic individuals if they have done something remarkable in our lives and their presence did mean a lot in the past.

Life is a rollercoaster, they say…

Life is an illusion too!

Sometimes to save a relationship, we need to apologize for somebody else's mistakes and there also comes a time where we need to simply move on. The law of nature teaches us to let go and it has ways to create a better version of ourselves. Some are just not designed for us.

My higher self felt it was absolutely okay to end such relations so to have inner peace.

All of us are judgmental. Experiences like these have taught me to be less critical. When I know nothing of what somebody else has gone through, it is best to shut my brain and mouth.

With numerous messages /calls, name calling and blame game, this had to end! I had to let go with grace and dignity.

Life is generous and kind to give us opportunities to shine and feel good about ourselves. I made use of this tough time to rise by getting myself involved in a charity drive. This kept me busy for straight 3 weeks from hereon. Connecting with long lost contacts was a delight and being of help to someone made me content. Bringing smiles and hope into someone's lives, eased my heart.

From nowhere, God blessed me with friend's who felt like family. Someone belonging to another country, speaking a different language, following a certain culture, yet the bond of friendship was stronger, connection was deeper with no strings of attachment. This lovely couple (Paolo and Coral) gave a beautiful definition of friendship through their genuineness and being a good example themselves. They buried the lousy feeling, poor brain functioning that 2020 murdered me with. Excitement and happiness overflowed which made few others question me if I was being emotional and not practical. I knew my life became happier, independent and I learned to value people. My good actions created good karma.

Part 8

BOOKS HAVE ALWAYS been the closest to my soul. The days when nothing seems to be working, I hug these pages tight and tuck them away. During this period, I got my hands on books like Mind Platter, Under Quarantine, The 5 AM Club. Reading nurtures my well-being and helps me think better. It was at this juncture, I felt the urge of writing something of my own. Through this book, I want the world to know what it is to feel free, pour out their vulnerability, be stronger in pain, take appropriate action, know that nothing lasts forever and life goes on, no matter what! How our lives must move on is a choice that we have.

Whenever I read inspirational stories about someone, I often think of what a beautiful soul that person is and if we have few more of such personalities this world would be a better place.

But now my thoughts have changed! Why do I urge people to be one of those beautiful souls? Why can't I be the one? Change must come from me rather than expecting it from others, except myself.

Countries fighting a war,

Leaving year's of violence and bloodshed,

History books bleeding with information on destruction,

Our generation surely ashamed of us for spreading hate,

Newspapers dropping the bombshell on their front pages,

Media with its debates,

You and I, nodding our heads when we hear of gruesome discoveries,

Don't you think our lives are pointless?

Don't you believe we have a higher potential to create a change?

What are we doing with our beautiful brain which is larger than our body?

Those billions of neurons seem to be sending signals to a wrong direction!

Let us wake up from our sleep,

Let us live our dreams,

Let us create a future of success and hope,

Let us be a reason to love.

If I need peace and happiness, I need to make a change. Change is uncomfortable because we do not think of giving it a try. We have created difficulties in our minds even before we experience the situation. If no one were ready to make alterations in their lifestyle and pattern of thinking, life would have been monotonous. Dreams would remain as dreams and life would no longer be exciting. People laugh at your dreams when they know it is a big one. Let them laugh, thank yourself for being a reason for them to laugh.

This reminds me of my childhood when I felt that the system of education was missing something in it and textbooks had information which lacked a form of interest. I started writing a letter addressing to the Head of the Education Department of the changes that need to be implemented so that the subject creates excitement for young minds to learn. I left the letter unfinished because I believed less and the fear of rejection was hanging on. My dream remained a dead one.

Our lives are filled with regrets because of us!

I regret the number of times I wanted to speak up at my workplace when I felt there was something wrong and unethical.

I wish I could go back and change what I wanted to do and say.

Do not let your wishes and dreams go unfulfilled by thinking it is too big and you are too small for it.

Part 9

UPS AND DOWNS are a part of life – Familiar?

So was the month of September.

First week brought the news of fright, terror and sadness when I heard that my husband met with an accident. He called me at 12:30 AM to share this sad news. He was calm but my voice quivered to hear that the car caught fire. I shook my head frantically.

There was a bigger miracle in this tragic incident.

My love was alive! Yes, Joy (my husband) was alive although he suffered minor injuries. But he was safe. Very often I forget to be thankful for the good that has taken place. It is a human life that counts. His silent prayers while driving to work gave him the strength to endure the loss.

There were memories attached to it,

Music that we listened to,

Long drives,
Shopping bags kept on the backseat,
Dates with our friend's,
Beverages gulped down in seconds,
Hugs and kisses shared,
Non stop chats until we reach the destination,
Getting lost on trial,

All of these were memories that we have had. The car was virtually reduced to ashes, but these memories live on.

This month reached its peak and I had enough. Weeks later, I felt a jolt in my heart and found myself perplexed. My voice choked with a feeling of heaviness within. I felt like cutting the blood supply and oxygen to my brain, because I could not endure this feeling any longer.

On a Monday, I texted my long distance best friend about the whole scenario that my mind was playing on. He came in with the best thought ever. His text read – "We cannot feel lonely if we are good with the person we are alone with, our own self. It is not the fault of the outside world. It is the strength that is missing within us. Find the strength within, feel the freedom."

These words created a major impact in my life. It changed me so much that I never look back after this day! I love myself, I am happy and grateful for the way I am. I now feel a deeper connection with myself. Nature, sunshine and rain embraced me. Meditation and yoga became a part of me. Through my eyes, I could feel the beauty of this world. Stronger connections with my loved one's added essence to life. I savored my few hour's of solitude and freedom every day onward.

When the outside world became too noisy with these ears turning deaf, my best friend saved my soul from giving up. God gives us the right people in our lives so to preserve and nurture such preciousness.

Part 10

PRACTICE AND PERSISTENCE is the key to everything. One of the definitive answers to my dilemma was to cut off from social media. The last 9 year's have been ridiculous as I was trying to get in line with other people, scrolling through the posts caused eye fatigue. I kept feeding my brain to incompetence. Of course there were positive thoughts, inspirational stories out there, which made me feel good for a short duration. Posting selfies, updating what my life is all about, displaying my frustration, reading comments and responding to them, posting comments on other profiles because I felt obliged to, made it all fancy, mentally deteriorating causing anxiety. It was about pleasing people who meant nothing to me. I was well aware that I was being silly and frivolous. It was almost as if I was stalling.

While social media does have its advantages for businessmen, author's, motivational speakers and to people who are in various professions, I was just being a little ant trying to make my way on a wrong platform. So I settled to plunge myself into something productive.

If I ever have to be there again, it has to be for a better purpose. This was my first step to freedom. I began to appreciate simple things, good friend's and real conversations. My heart opened its way to peace and I could feel a strong rhythm of faith. I experienced the importance of practicing gratitude.

Grateful for this mystery in my life,
For I know my clan,
My soul is now free from evil.
Grateful for these 4 corners of the wall,
They keep me safe,
Protecting me from every harm,
I can now meditate deeply.
Grateful for my loving family and beautiful friend's,
My mum, an angel gifted forever,
For her sacrifice and love,
The promises that she never breaks,
For her care and warmth,
In every thing she does.
Grateful to be able to breathe.
The past is gone,
The future remains a mystery.

I know nothing of what Christmas will look like this year,
But my heart is filled with love,
My home is filled with light,
My Christmas will be filled with cheer.
I now reminisce my past, dream of my love,
Of how we used to soak up the sun,
With dinner's at the beach,
Walking in the empty moonlit streets,
Some places being our secret getaway,
Those days filled with passion and laughter.
Dropping me off,
Kissing me goodbye,
Midnight calls which lasted until we greeted our sweet morning's,
Grateful to have experienced this love.
The present has been blessed,
With dear friend's for a lifetime,
Teaching me to free my mind,
To love endlessly,
Letting me know that distance never matters,
When our hearts are filled with love and warmth,
Grateful for their trust in me.
My home is filled with the sweetest music,
Of giggles and funny little noises,
My tiny human who fills the void,
With the sound of her laugh,

Cutest way of saying certain words,
The unique person she is growing into,
Her pride when she shows something new,
The way her hand fits in mine,
I pause and breathe slow,
For these are ecstatic moments to cherish.
Gratefulness is tattooed within me.
You can now see the stars in my eyes,
Feel the fire in my veins,
My heart shines brighter than the sun,
You will only find a work of art in me.
I see the beauty in my soul,
I feel the love in your heart.

Part 11

MY EXPERIENCES RESONATE powerfully with a lot of people in different ways. May this episode in our lives bring out the best in us. Let us be able to encircle ourselves with the power of hope. The day we get those masks off our faces, let our faces shine with a smile and carry gratitude in our hearts. We are gifted with a life that is created out of love. Let us not live with hate in our hearts.

Deeply grateful to my loving family – Joy, Jazlyn, my dearest Mom and my forever friend's who are family – Karyn, Shanti, Divya, Coral, Paolo.

Grateful to this most powerful human, my virtual mentor – Taarika. You light up my life.

Each one of you are unique and distinctively beautiful.

Thank you for enriching my life beyond measure, with your presence.

You are the roots that continue to give me wings.

You all have been a huge mirror through which I could see myself clearly and authentically.

A text saying just a "Hi" brings in radiance and joy in my heart. I value your time and appreciate your selflessness.

I am forever grateful for the love, joy, laughter and friendship that you all bring to my life.

You are rare and treasured group of souls.

Oh 2020! – Please know you are the best too! You have added long lasting fragrance to my life.

Printed by Libri Plureos GmbH in Hamburg,
Germany